Scattered throughout New England there are thousands of stone walls
crisscrossing woods and fields as if they have been there forever.
Each one has a story to tell, a story of farmers and oxen and hard, muddy work.
And every stone in every wall also has a story to tell, an older story
of the land itself, of mountains and glaciers, of soils and seas.

STONE

WALL

SECRETS

Kristine and Robert Thorson

Illustrated by Gustav Moore

TILBURY HOUSE PUBLISHERS GARDINER MAINE

The old man stood on the porch of the shuttered white farmhouse. With his strong, tough hands he gently unfolded the letter and read it once again. The letter asked him to sell the stones, the ones from the farmstead walls. He folded the paper again. Distracted, he ran his fingertips along the creased edge.

"Should I sell the walls, or not?" he asked himself. He could certainly use the extra money. Besides, the walls weren't being used for anything. So why did he feel so reluctant to sell the stones? Why did he feel so sad about letting them disappear from his land forever?

He stepped off the porch onto the dew-covered grass. "I wonder what Adam will think?" His soft, intelligent eyes scanned the road expectantly, but there was no sign of his grandson. He strolled to the garden to wait, settling comfortably into the cushioned wooden swing the boy had helped paint last spring. It rocked him gently, body and mind—back and forth, back and forth—through space and through time.

His thoughts drifted back to earlier days when he and his sister were young. Oh, how they loved to play on the walls! In summer, they saddled stone ponies for a circus parade. In autumn, the wall was a pirate ship to sail on a sea of gold and red leaves. In winter, the stones became monsters with icicle teeth. And, in the spring, they jumped aboard their Stone Wall Express and chugged away to a far-off land.

A familiar voice interrupted his happy memories, abruptly pulling him back to the present. "Hey, Grampa!" shouted Adam, squealing his bicycle to a halt. The boy hopped off and shoved his bike against the barn. "What did you want?" he asked, gulping air in great breaths.

"Your help," replied Grampa, who had walked out to greet him. "And something more important—your opinion." Grampa really did value his grandson's opinion. After all, the farm would someday be his.

The boy, breathing more easily, quizzically raised one eyebrow. "My opinion? About what?"

"Our walls," answered Grampa mysteriously. "Our stone walls." He watched the expression on his grandson's face change from curiosity to bewilderment. All Adam had been told was to come prepared for a long day of work.

The old man hesitated. And then he told Adam their dilemma. A stonemason was offering to buy the stones from the family's old walls. He wanted to take the stones from the walls, toss them into a truck, and haul them to the city where they could be built into grander walls around fancier houses. And he was willing to pay a fair price, just to take the stones.

"I don't see any problem," said Adam, pointing to one of the walls, half-hidden in weeds. "Nobody here needs those old rocks anymore. Why not get rid of them and make some money, too?"

"I wish it were that simple for me." Grandpa sighed. "Come on. I've got something to show you. And we have some walls to inspect."

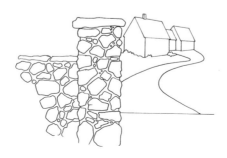

The autumn weather was warm, the ground firm and dry. It was the perfect time to tour the old farm and patch any walls needing repair—a chore that Grampa had always loved to do. Usually only a stone or two would slip to one side, jostled by frost or the roots of a tree. But once in a while, a short stretch of wall would collapse and need to be rebuilt.

Grampa and Adam followed a well-worn path through ghosts of pastures now thick with pine. They hiked first through the small orchard, loading their pockets with fruit plucked from gnarled limbs. But along each wall, they slowed their pace, stopping now and then to return a fallen stone to its rightful place.

After a while, Grampa paused to sink his still-strong teeth into a juicy red apple. The golden September sun warmed him, gently soothing his spirit. The questions that troubled him, about selling the stones, faded away. Adam, lingering nearby, leaned down. From the moss-covered ground he picked up a white, grainy stone.

"Ahh—where do you think that stone came from?" quizzed Grampa.

Adam faced his grandfather with a puzzled frown. "From the wall, Grampa, just like the others," he answered, not quite sure what the old man meant.

Grampa grinned. He reached for the small, white stone, lifting it high into the sunlight, where it sparkled in front of the boy's brown eyes. Then the old man began his story—a stone wall story—one that took them back through time.

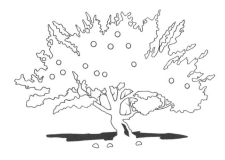

Look closely," said Grampa, offering the stone to the boy. "See what's trapped inside."

Adam turned the grainy stone in his hands like a kaleidoscope, squinting from the reflected sunlight. He glanced up at Grampa, then down at the stone, then back up again, not knowing what to say next. Finally, he saw what had been there all along, grains of clean sand, now frozen within the stone.

"Looks like sand to me," said the boy quietly, still unsure of himself.

"Right!" confirmed Grampa. "It's beach sand. From an ancient ocean that was here, right here, a very long time ago."

"Here?" protested Adam. "Here on this hill?" He tried to imagine foaming waves crashing there on that quiet, forested hillside. But he couldn't. "That's impossible!"

"Is it?" replied Grampa. "The proof is in your hand." The old man licked his lips as if to taste the salty spray—then continued.

Those sand grains were part of a beach that lay at the edge of a vast sea, half a billion years ago. And in that sea swam primitive fish, like armored monsters on patrol. They swam past colorful corals that swayed like coconut trees. Mud and sand settled downward—slowly, steadily, silently—in that ancient undersea world."

Grampa looked up. A flock of honking geese flew through the clear, blue sky towards the other side of the valley. He blinked. The birds and sky vanished. The air was an ocean; the birds, a school of fish, swimming, swimming in a deep blue sea.

E ons passed," he went on, now pointing at the opposite ridge. "The mud and sand were buried deep within the earth. There, miles below the surface, heat and pressure, bit by bit, baked the mud into slabby, gray rock—rock that now fills all these walls." Grampa waved his arm in a wide arc.

Adam waited until Grampa turned away. Then he slipped the grainy, white stone into his pocket, like a paperback book to be read on a rainy day. Using both hands, he tipped up a heavy gray slab of stone. He noticed its many layers—some milky white, others black with speckles. The young one said nothing while he traced the layers with his fingers and listened to the old one's tale.

"Earthquakes rumbled, thrusting the mud into mountains. Volcanoes fumed. The smell of sulfur—like rotten eggs—spewed into the air."

Grampa inhaled deeply as if to sniff the ancient air. Adam dropped the heavy slab. It landed in the soil with a thud. "Wait a minute, Grampa," he said. "First you claimed the rock was ocean mud. Now you say it came from a mountain?"

"It may sound confusing," said Grampa, "but it's true. The mass of layered rock formed first. Then, two continents rammed into each other, pushing the layers higher and higher until gigantic mountain ranges appeared. But mountains come and mountains go. Making them is the easy part; getting rid of them is much harder. Nature needs time, lots of time, for the sun, the wind, and the rain to break the rocks apart and send them to the sea."

I 'll show you what I mean," said the old man. Without another word, Grampa squatted down to study the nearby wall. He lifted stone after stone, pausing now and then to flip one over.

"I've got one!"

"Got what?" asked Adam.

"Here, have a look for yourself." Grampa stepped back.

Adam noticed the pebbles right away. The way they stuck out of the brown, muddy sand reminded him of peanut brittle—except that these "nuts" were different sizes and colors. "It's gravel, isn't it? But it's as hard as cement!"

"You're right," said Grampa. "But this gravel has been cemented by time, deep within the earth. The pebbles began their journey in a mountain stream. They bounced along the river beds towards a distant sea, growing rounder and smoother with every mile. All these pebbles eventually washed together to form an ancient gravel, which we can see in this rock today."

Grampa stood silent and still in the shade of the trees. The breeze, blowing through the autumn leaves, seemed like the rush of a distant river, echoing up from the valley below. The fluttering sound of leaves became the muffled sound of pebbles, bumping each other beneath the flowing water. Adam, too, said nothing.

A few moments passed before they resumed their hike along the trail. The path sloped gently, higher and higher, until it reached an overlook where they could gaze upon the farm and fields below. It had always been Grampa's favorite spot. There, at the edge of his land, tucked into the corner of a wall, he had stored a special stone.

R eaching below the silken cobwebs, Grampa pulled out a smooth, black stone covered with tiny scratches. "This stone tells one of my favorite stories—the story of the great Ice Age. Twenty thousand years ago, a giant glacier oozed southward over all New England, smothering even the tallest mountains with ice. On top, the glacier was a snowflake desert: frigid, white, and blinding beneath a brilliant sun. On the bottom, the ice lay in total darkness; it pressed the brittle, broken rock back into hard mud." Grampa suddenly felt very cold. Adam shivered.

"Feel these scratches," urged Grampa as he blew away dust from the stone. Adam rubbed his fingers over the shallow grooves on the dark polished surface. "Can you imagine the grip of that glacier, the grating and grinding of stone against ledge?"

Adam shivered. He knew the sound of two stones scraping together, but what would that sound like beneath a mile of ice?

The old man continued. "The glacier streamed by for thousands of years. The climate warmed; the ice changed to muddy water and then disappeared, leaving behind a windy, treeless world. The dust from dried-up rivers choked the air."

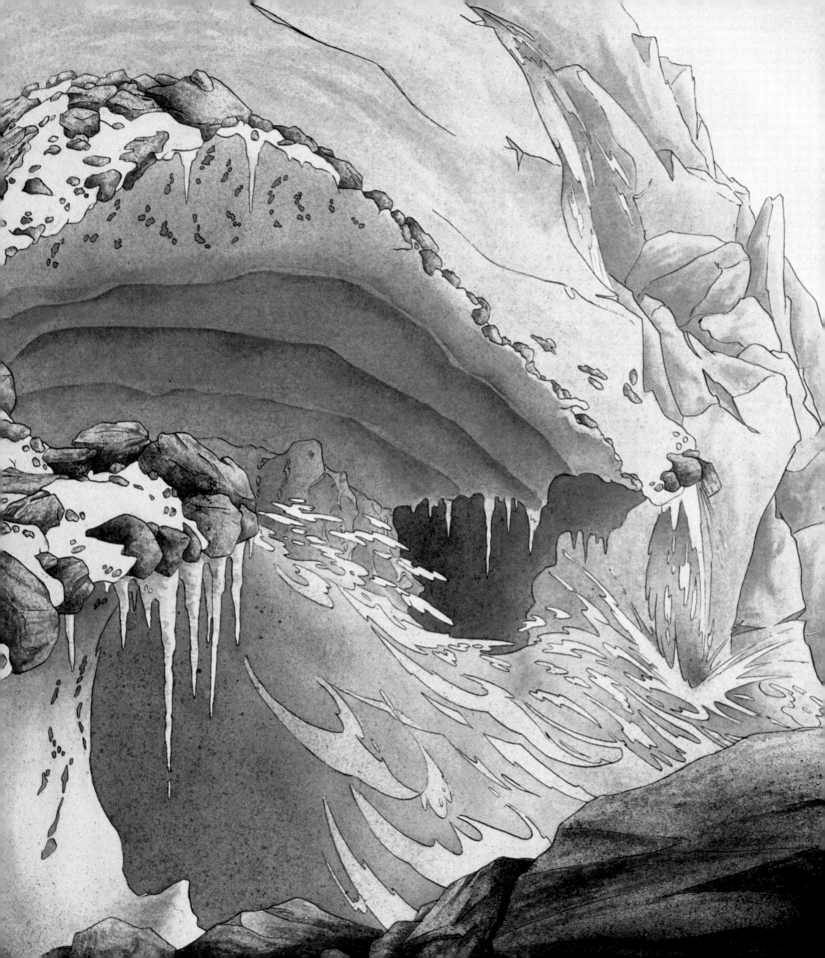

Grampa paused, transported far, far back in time. He could hear the frigid water rushing through icy caverns. He could see the glacier melting, leaving the land behind bleak and bare and brown. He could feel the gusty winds swirling all around him. He gasped for breath as if he were really there, watching the dust settle back to a rocky, rubbled earth.

"Are you all right?" asked Adam, worried by Grampa's sudden wheezing breaths.

"Oh, yes, I'm fine." Grampa eyed the boy uncertainly. "Sometimes those ancient worlds seem so real to me—as rich in sights and sounds and smells as our present world," he confessed. "As if I'd been there once and could go there again. But, of course, that's not possible, is it?" Grampa stopped. His grandson stood speechless.

Grampa cleared his throat. "Then, out of the dust sprang a spongy green carpet of plants called tundra. Tiny flowers and miniature shrubs hugged the ground in that cooler, windier world. Caribou grazed in great herds. Woolly brown mammoths trampled the tundra, waving their trunks in the air."

Grampa, with a far-away look in his eyes, cupped his hands behind his ears. "Can you hear them?" he whispered to the boy.

"Hear what?" whispered Adam back, cupping his ears like the old man.

"The mammoths," murmured Grampa. The oddest expression crossed over Adam's face. He quickly dropped his hands from his head. For a second, he almost believed that he had heard something, too.

"The tundra receded northward when the climate began to warm. The animals migrated, too, leaving bleached antlers and tusks behind. The trees returned—first spruce and pine, next birch and oak, then finally, all the rest. Their roots cracked the hard, glacial soil, breaking it apart. Dust and leaves mixed together with stones and sand to make a rich, dark soil. The forest filled with woodland creatures—wolves, bears, panthers, possums, and deer."

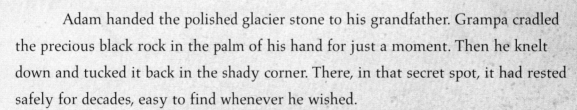

Adam handed the polished glacier stone to his grandfather. Grampa cradled the precious black rock in the palm of his hand for just a moment. Then he knelt down and tucked it back in the shady corner. There, in that secret spot, it had rested safely for decades, easy to find whenever he wished.

Grampa stood up straight, strangely content. He saw that Adam was staring off into space, still and quiet, as if in a trance. Grampa wondered, "Was I right to hope that he's ready to learn—to read the stones, to travel through time, to hear the earth as it speaks to me?"

Wordlessly, the two headed through woods toward the opposite corner of the abandoned meadow. Along the way, a giant green hemlock lay uprooted, completely blocking the path. Grampa detoured deeper into the woods around the tangled, soil-clinging roots. Adam chose a different path; he scrambled up on a nearby stone wall, following it like a rocky road. The stones shifted beneath his feet, so he concentrated on each step, never losing his balance. He was about to jump down when something out of the ordinary caught his eye. It was a stone, dull and dusky red on one side, gray on the other. He slid off the wall, lifted the unusual stone with both hands, and lugged it to the nearby path. "What's this?" he demanded, dropping it on the grass in front of his grandfather.

Grampa bent down for a closer look. "That's a campfire stone. See how it has been scorched rusty red on the outside, then shattered by the fire's heat?"

Adam flipped the stone over in the grass, examining each side.

Grampa explained with a touch of excitement, "This rock tells many tales. Its crystals are ancient, millions of years old. Its shape is glacial, from the last ice age. And its home is now a wall built two centuries ago."

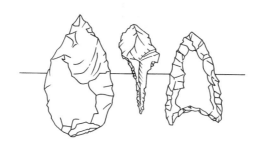

B ut what about the campfire? When was that?" interrupted Adam.
"Sometime after the ice. Exactly when, I don't know. But people did live
here. They crouched around a crackling fire, heating their hands near the
flames. And, if they were lucky, they breathed in air that smelled of roasting
meat and corn, while their children played nearby. They sang their songs, they
told their tales, uttering sounds and sentences lost to a misty past. But they left
this special stone behind, and it speaks for them today."

Adam already knew about the Indians who were here when the Pilgrims
landed. He had read about their villages of bark-covered longhouses, and
about their clothing and canoes. He also knew something about their ancient
ancestors, the original Americans, who had lived here for hundreds of
generations before the written word.

Adam had learned about this earlier story from his mother's collection
of stone artifacts, which she had recently given to a museum. What he now
realized was that these primitive tools were also special stones, fashioned not
by ancient beaches or grinding glaciers, but by people long ago.

The oldest tools in her collection were like long flint knives. They were
used by nomads—Paleoindians—who ambushed caribou with their stone-tipped
spears in an almost-tundra world. Next came village-dwellers—Archaics—who
hunted deer with bow and arrow, and who speared fish in flowing streams.
Finally came the larger tribes—Woodland Indians—who planted crops with
blunt stone hoes and who stewed their food in fired clay pots.

The ancestors of Adam's adoptive family, and other settlers, were next in line. They also left their stones and tools and bones. Of course, they left a written history too, so more is known about them. These colonists from Europe changed the wilderness from forest into farm. They chopped down acre after acre of tall timber, burning the trees in bonfires that glowed orange and red through long days and nights. Oxen bellowed and clanked their chains as they tore the stumps from the ground. Man and beast worked as a team to change the world forever.

Holding his red-scorched stone with both hands, Adam headed back to the wall. He searched for a gap where his prize could be safely hidden, as though it were a precious relic. Within a minute he was back on the path with his grandfather. They walked side by side, stopping here and there to patch the wall with fallen stone.

The old meadow rose high enough so that they could see the landscape below them. Hunting parties no longer traveled through primeval forests; instead, a patchwork of former farms with stone-rimmed fields covered the countryside.

"Did you build any of those walls all by yourself?" asked Adam. He hadn't realized how many stone walls existed in their little corner of the earth.

"Just those two—the ones near the pond," answered the old man wistfully, pointing his arm like a rifle. "But, of course, I helped build others, adding my stones to the ones already there."

Scenes from his childhood flashed through his mind, sparked by the sight of the walls he helped build. The farm had been a busy place then, with its grassy green pastures dotted large with cows and small with sheep. The corn rustled tall in the summer breeze, growing so fast that it squeaked. Pumpkin leaves smothered the ground with humid shade. Apple trees dropped their juicy gifts from above. And the barn stood red and straight, stuffed full of sweet-smelling hay.

Grandfather and grandson worked their way downhill, stopping here and there to stack loose stones back in place. Within minutes, however, they discovered a tumbled section of the wall that needed to be rebuilt. At first, Adam thought the job was impossible, because the stones kept sliding back down, almost smashing his toes. But soon he learned the trick. He laid one stone on two, and two on one, layer after layer. He chinked them up on the outside so they tilted towards the middle.

"Looks like that will hold for now," said the boy proudly as he hefted a stone to the top of the wall. That finished the job, so he turned away from Grampa, who was on the other side of the wall. Moments later, from behind him came the crashing sound of falling stones. Adam whirled around, eyes wide with surprise. There, on the ground, lay the last of the stones he had just replaced. "I'll have to square them away more carefully this time," he scolded himself. That's when the old one decided to pop up from behind the wall, grinning mischievously from ear to ear. Adam realized immediately that he'd been tricked! Grampa himself had knocked over the stones.

"Grampa!" he wailed, in exasperation.

"All right, all right!" Grampa chuckled. Then the two of them quickly set to work repairing the fallen stones. He didn't tell Adam that someone had played the same joke on him a half century earlier. Before long, they lifted the last stone into place. Their tour through time was nearly done, but Grampa had saved something wonderful for the way home. With the old man in the lead, they set off in the direction of the farmhouse, stopping in a field deeply shaded by paper birches.

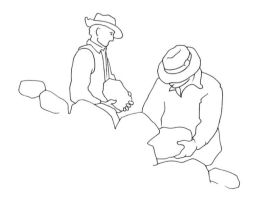

S tones, like those the stonemason hoped to buy, bordered the former pasture. Beginning in one corner, Grampa marched like a stiff-legged soldier, thirty-two paces beside the wall, beckoning Adam to follow. He explained nothing. He simply directed Adam to help him clear away a pile of rotting brush, promising mysteriously that it would prove worthwhile. Adam's arms began to ache, and he was about to complain when an astonishing sight froze the words in his throat.

"Is it what I think it is? A meteorite?" asked Adam. He had seen a meteorite before, on a school trip to the planetarium. His hands touched the cold, pitted surface of a half-buried boulder, partly hidden by ferns.

"Exactly," said the old man proudly as if it were the largest diamond in the world. "This boulder is a family secret. It once was a shooting star. You can see where the metal melted and bubbled as it burned its way to the ground."

"I wish I could have seen it fall!" cried Adam, automatically shifting his gaze skyward.

"It fell long before your time, or mine," said Grampa. "But not here. The glacier carried it from someplace else, maybe a hundred miles away, and dumped it here on our land. It might have even landed hot on the ice, before being buried in the snow. I reckon a museum would pay a hefty sum for such a fine specimen."

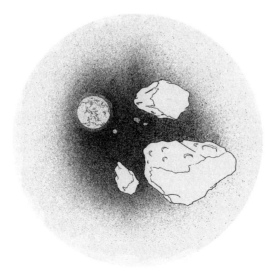

Grampa leaned back against the bronze-black rock, letting the sunbeams soak in. He shut his eyes, reminded of that clear August evening with his sister when streaks of stardust blazed through the dark night sky. It was there, flat on his back in the field by the pond, that he had watched his first meteor shower, awestruck. There were so many stars—too many to count—and they were so very far away.

That night his sister pointed at a distant spot in the sky. She told him that he'd been born out there and then brought to earth by a falling star. He was so young then, he almost believed her. In fact, she insisted he owed his life to the shooting stars. Later, much later, he learned that his sister's ideas weren't really so far-fetched, that every atom in his body had first arrived on earth that same way.

Grampa explained this all to Adam. Keeping his eyes closed to protect them from the sunlight, the old man spoke about the sun, the moon, the stars, and how everything all began. How fragments like their meteorite collided and crashed and collected in space until all the planets were born. How leftover pieces still in orbit will fall for eons to come. How a meteorite miles across slammed into the earth ending, some say, the reign of the dinosaurs. And, finally, how someday, perhaps, another big one may fall, bringing unknown changes to a future world.

A little later, when he slowly opened his eyes, Grampa realized he was alone. Had his words gone unheard?

From a distance, Adam called out loudly. Grampa hurried
onward until he arrived at an old storage shed that sagged
under the weight of a century. Adam was standing inside on a
stout, wooden sled.

"Look," said Adam. "It's your stone boat, Grampa."

Grampa paused for a moment. The sled was full of
memories, instead of stones.

"I remember the day when my sister and I helped
Great-Uncle Cyrus clear the fields—a chore he did each spring.
We hitched horses to this boat, and headed for the open fields.
There, in an ocean of mud, we fished out stone after stone, and
thunked 'em down. When the pile was high enough, we
climbed aboard before Cyrus shouted, 'Gid-up now. Go, Sue!'
Then away we went, skidding and slipping to the edge of the
field. I was the captain, docking a boat filled with a harvest of
stone.

"Then, while the horses caught their breath, we jumped
off the boat, picked up the stones, and stacked them into place,
one by one. Big ones on the bottom, small ones on top."

"Why did you pick just a few loads each year?" asked Adam.

"I asked the same thing myself when I was a boy," replied Grampa. "And I didn't get much of an answer. During lunch with the men in the field—milk, cornbread, and strawberry jam—Cyrus told me that there weren't many stones in the early years. And then, suddenly, stones started popping up everywhere. Some folks thought the Devil had put them in the ground. Other folks swore that the stones sprouted from seed. You know what they called them? New England potatoes!"

Grampa laughed. He then told Adam what happened. With the trees gone, the topsoil thinned and the ground froze deeper than ever before. Left by the glacier, stones that hadn't seen the light of day for thousands of years heaved to the surface and had to be hauled away. Like the farmers before him, Grampa had to put the stones somewhere, so he, too, stacked them onto walls. As the walls rose up, they became more than long piles of stone. Some walls divided fields while others marked boundary lines. Some grew high enough to fence in wayward sheep or cows. The nicest walls—those near the house—were works of art. Every wall had a story of its own.

"Let's get on home," suggested Grampa as Adam jumped off the stone boat. "I'm hungry. It's awfully late for lunch."

They left the musty shed behind and followed a sun-dappled path towards home. Adam began to notice how many different kinds of walls there were. Square flat stones built tall straight walls. Rounded ones made tumbled rows. Sometimes the stones were black or rust or white or silver, but most were plain and gray. Crusty lichens and velvety moss colored the stones with patches of yellow and green. Birds and bugs, squirrels and spiders, chipmunks and children—every creature loved the old stone walls.

The pair wandered along the forest path, the younger following in the footsteps of the older one. With each step, the lessons of the day became clearer to Adam, taking root more firmly than either of them could have predicted. Grampa had been showing him something important all morning: that the past, the present, and the future were alive in every stone; that his history, his family's history, and the history of the peoples who'd lived here before them were connected to the stones.

The walls were like a library, stacked high with earthen books. Each stone contained a story of time and place now gone—an older story of oceans, mountains, glaciers, and native peoples who left their mark on the land. And each wall also told a younger story—of Yankee pioneers and those who followed, like Grampa, and Adam himself.

When they reached the porch, Grampa stopped to look back at the land that he loved. He pulled the letter from his pocket, unfolded it, and held it out to his grandson.

"Well, young man," he said. "What's your advice? Should we sell our walls, or not?"

Adam had completely forgotten about the stonemason's letter. His eyes swept

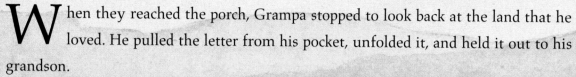

the hills and fields, trying to picture them barren of walls, like libraries without books.

Earlier that very day, he had answered the same question so easily. If someone wanted to pay good money for a pile of old stones, he had thought, then why not? But now Adam wasn't so sure. He couldn't find the right words to reply.

He reached out for the letter that Grampa was holding and read it for the very first time. He folded it thoughtfully and pushed it deep into his pocket.

"I'm thirsty," said Adam. "Any of that cold cider left in the kitchen?"

"Let's go find out," replied Grampa.

The old man placed his arm around his grandson's shoulders, and together they went inside.

Tilbury House, Publishers
132 Water Street
Gardiner, Maine 04345

First printing: July 1998

10 9 8 7 6 5 4 3 2 1

Cataloging-in-Publication Data
Thorson, Kristine.
        Stone wall secrets / Kristine and Robert Thorson : illustrated by Gustav Moore.
        p. cm.
        Summary: As he and his grandson walk along the stone walls surrounding his New England farm, an old man shares stories about the geologic history of the stones as well as some of the memories they hold for him.
        ISBN 0-88448-195-6 (alk. paper)
        [1. Rocks--Fiction. 2. Grandfathers--Fiction. 3. New England--fiction.] I. Thorson, Robert M., 1951–   . II. Moore, Gustav, ill.   III. Title.
PZ7.T3993St. 1998
p[Fic.]--dc21   97-49982
                                                                 CIP
                                                                 AC

Illustrations by Gustav Moore, Portland, Maine.
Design and Layout: Geraldine Millham, Westport, Massachusetts.
Editorial and Production: Jennifer Elliott, Diane Vinal, and Barbara Diamond.
Color Scans and Film: Integrated Composition Systems, Spokane, Washington.
Printing and Binding: Worzalla Publishing, Stevens Point, Wisconsin.

Also Available:
STONE WALL SECRETS TEACHER'S GUIDE: EXPLORING GEOLOGY IN THE CLASSROOM
Ruth Deike
Paperback, $9.95   ISBN 0-88448-196-4
8¹/₂ x 11, 80 pages, illustrations   Education/Science; Grades 3–6

Ruth Deike, a geologist with the U. S. Geologic Survey for more than thirty years and the founder of The Rock Detective, a non-profit educational organization, brings boundless energy to teaching school children about earth science. Her Teacher's Guide incorporates the imagery and wonder of *Stone Wall Secrets* with hands-on classroom activities that illustrate basic earth science concepts. Ruth has learned that what young Rock Detectives discover for themselves, they remember. Working with the National Science Education Standards, she has created a variety of exciting activities, from exploring the earth's building blocks, to studying volcanoes to posing intriguing questions such as, Does the earth itch? Or, Will there be another ice age?